103221

For Kate -D.B.

To Louis, with love -Rosi x

tiger tales
an imprint of ME Media, LLC
202 Old Ridgefield Road, Wilton, CT 06897
Published in the United States 2009
Originally published in Great Britain 2009
by Egmont UK Limited
Text copyright © David Bedford 2009
Illustrations copyright © Rosalind Beardshaw 2009
CIP data is available
Printed in Singapore
Hardcover ISBN-13: 978-1-58925-084-0
Hardcover ISBN-10: 1-58925-084-2
Paperback ISBN-13: 978-1-58925-417-6
Paperback ISBN-10: 1-58925-417-1
All rights reserved
1 3 5 7 9 10 8 6 4 2

Mole's

in Love

by David Bedford

Illustrated by Rosalind Beardshaw

tiger tales

One bright day, Morris the mole peeped out of his hole to find that it was spring.

"Yippee!" said Morris.

Then he hopped
down from his hill
and went off to find
someone to love.

Morris peered
around the farm.

Moles don't see very well. But
Morris didn't think it would be hard
to find someone to love because he
knew just what to look for. . . .

Shiny black fur.

Luscious shiny black fur!

Morris hugged the Luscious Shiny Black Fur. **He was** *in love!* Morris blew his love a kiss.

But when the Luscious Shiny Black Fur blew him a kiss back . . .

Morris was blown off his feet!

He landed in a pile of leaves—but nobody came to see if he was all right.

Then Morris smelled the first new flowers of spring.

"**Yippee!**" he said, and he skipped out of the leaves and went off to find someone else to love.

"**Ouch!**" Morris said to himself, feeling glum.

A pink nose.

A pretty pink nose!

Morris hugged the
Pretty Pink Nose.
He was
in love!
Morris rubbed his
love's nose.

But when the
Pretty Pink Nose
rubbed back . . .

Morris was sent rolling away,

cold and wet and slimy
from head to toe!

Then he heard
the happy twitter
of birds singing
about spring.

"Yippee!" said Morris, and he jumped
out of the mud and went to find someone
else to love.

He landed in some mud—but nobody
came to see if he was all right.
"Ouch," Morris said to himself,
feeling glum.

Big

wide

feet.

Gorgeous
big wide
feet!

Morris hugged the
Gorgeous Big Wide Feet.
He was
in love!
Morris sat down in the
meadow with his love.

But when the
Gorgeous Big Wide
Feet sat down, too...

Morris was

choked and tickled by feathers.

"**Ah-choo!**" he sneezed, tumbling backward.

This time he landed on a sharp thistle—but
nobody came to see if he was all right.
"**Ouch,**" Morris said to himself, feeling
glummer than ever. "**Ouch, ouch, OUCH!**"

And even though he knew it was still spring,
he went back and sat on his molehill.

Morris said to himself, "It is spring and I am alone without love.
Luscious Shiny Black Fur was too rough.
Pretty Pink Nose was too wet.
And **Gorgeous Big Wide Feet** made
me sneeze.

I looked for love and didn't find it."

Suddenly, Morris heard a tiny
voice. It said,

"You have not looked hard enough!"

And before he could blink . . .

someone gave him
a **present**.

The present balanced
on his nose

and wrapped
around his ears.

And when Morris
looked **through**
his present, he saw
very clearly...

Luscious Shiny Black Fur.

A Pretty Pink Nose.

Gorgeous Big Wide Feet,

and best of all,

Perfect Sparkly Eyeglasses!

"My name is Mini," said the tiny voice, as Morris stared down at her. **"Are you all right?"**

And Morris said,

"Yes, I **am!**"

Morris hopped down from his hill. But he wasn't looking for love anymore.

♡ Love had ♡
already found him.